The Scream

Rohinton Mistry

illustrations by Tony Urquhart

McCLELLAND & STEWART

*Originally published in a special limited edition of 150
for World Literacy of Canada in 2006.*

LIBRARY AND ARCHIVES CANADA CATALOGUING IN PUBLICATION

Mistry, Rohinton, 1952-
    The scream / Rohinton Mistry ; illustrated by Tony Urquhart.
ISBN 978-0-7710-6132-5

I. Urquhart, Tony II. Title.

PS8576.I853S38 2008   c813´.54   c2008-901952-0

We acknowledge the financial support of the Government of Canada through the
Book Publishing Industry Development Program and that of the Government of
Ontario through the Ontario Media Development Corporation's Ontario Book
Initiative. We further acknowledge the support of the Canada Council for the
Arts and the Ontario Arts Council for our publishing program.

PRINTED AND BOUND IN CANADA

This book was produced using ancient-forest friendly papers.

McClelland & Stewart Ltd.
75 Sherbourne Street, Toronto, Ontario, M5A 2P9
www.mcclelland.com

1   2   3   4   5   12   11   10   09   08

For Freny

THE SCREAM

THE FIRST TIME I HEARD
the scream outside my
window, I had just fallen asleep.
It was many nights ago. The sound pierced the
darkness like a needle. Behind it, it pulled an
invisible thread of pain.

The night was suffocating, I remember. There
was no sign of rain. The terrible cry disturbed
the dry, dusty air, then died in silence. Bullies,
torturers, executioners all prefer silence.
Exceptions are made for the sounds of their
instruments, their grunts of effort, their victims'
agony. The rest is silence. No wisdom like
silence. Silence is golden. I associated silence
with virtuous people. Or at least harmless,
inoffensive people. I was thinking of Trappist

1

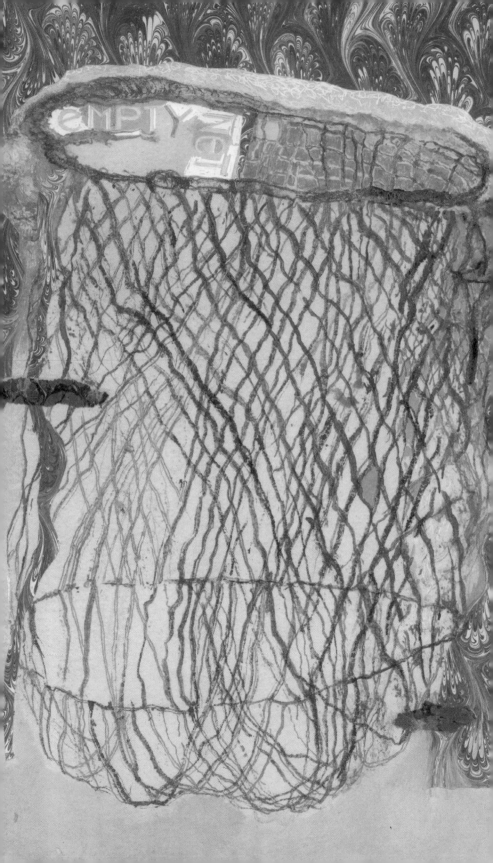

monks, of gurus and babas who take vows of silence. I was wrong. Even at my great age, there are things to learn.

The scream disturbed none in the flat. No one opened a window and poked out a curious head. The buildings across the road were hushed as well. The light of the street lamp grew dimmer. No witnesses?

Could I have dreamt it? But the scream was followed by shrieks: Bachaaav, bachaav! yelled the man, help me, please! I opened my eyes, and there were more screams. Frightened, I shut my eyes. It was utterly horripilating. I was afraid to rise and look out the window. He begged them to stop hitting, to please forgive: Mut maaro, maaf karo!

That was nights ago. But when it gets dark and the light is switched off, I can think of nothing else. If I do think of something else, sooner or later the scream returns. It comes like a disembodied hand to clutch my throat and choke my windpipe. Then it is difficult to fall asleep, especially at my age, with my many worries. Signs of trouble are everywhere. The seagulls keep screeching. The seedlings are wilting and ready to die. The fishermen's glistening nets emerge from the sea, emptier than yesterday. All day long there is shouting and fighting. Buses and lorries thunder past. Mediocre politicians make loud speeches, bureaucrats wag arrogant fingers, fanatics howl blood-curdling threats. And even at night there is no peace.

I sleep on a mattress on the floor, in the front room. In the front room the light is better. The dust lies thick on the furniture. The others use the back room. My place too used to be there, among them. All night long I would hear their orchestra of wind instruments, their philharmonia of dyspepsia, when, with the switching off of the lights, it was as if a conductor had raised his baton and given the downbeat, for it started immediately, the snoring, wheezing, sighing, coughing, belching, and farting. Not that I was entirely silent myself. But at least my age gives me the right; pipes grown old cannot remain

soundless. In that caliginous back room, verging on the hypogean, with its dark nooks and corners, often the air would be inspissated before half the night was through. And yet, it was so much better than being alone, so comforting to lie amidst warm, albeit noisy, bodies when one's own grew less and less warm, day by day.

Horripilating. Caliginous. Hypogean. Inspissated. It pleases me that these words are not lost on you. Well may you wonder why I use them, when equivalents of the common or garden variety would do. Patience, I am no show-off. Though I will readily admit that if gems like these sit unused inside me for too long, they make me costive. A periodic purge is essential for an old man's well-being. At my age, well-being is a relative concept. So I repeat, I am no exhibitionist, this is not a manifestation of logorrhoea or wanton sesquipedalianism. At my age, there is no future in showing off. There are good reasons. Patience.

All my life I have feared mice, starvation, and

loneliness. But now that loneliness has arrived, it's not so bad. What could I do, the others no longer wanted me among them, in the back room. I suppose I was a nuisance. Hence my mattress on the floor, in the front room, wedged between the sofa and the baby grand. I am in a tight spot. One wrong turn and I could bruise a knee or crack my forehead. The others were only too glad to see me go. They began laying out the stained and lumpy mattress for me each night. Once, I pointed to the servant and said to them, "Let him carry it."

"He is not a servant, he is our son," they said, "don't you recognize your own grandchild?"

Such liars. Such lies they tell me, to make me think I am losing my mind. And they carry my mattress, wearing their supererogatory airs, as if concerned about an old man's welfare. But I know the truth hidden in their hearts. They are poor actors. They think at my age I can no longer separate the genuine from the spurious, the real from the acted, so why bother with elaborate efforts to dissimulate. They will learn, when they are old like me, that untangling the enemy's skein of deceit becomes easier as time goes by.

With your permission, I will give you an example. Sometimes I find it difficult to rise from my chair. So I call the servant: "Chhokra, give me a hand." If his masters are not watching, he comes at once. If they are, he ignores me, naturally, not wanting to cross them. Taking a leaf from their book, he even mocks me. I wonder why they spoil him so much. Good servants are hard to find, yes. But to let him eat with them at table? Sleep in the same room, on a mahogany four-poster? And for me a mattress flung across the floor. What days have come. Kaliyug is indeed upon us. It's a world gone arsy-versy.

After moving to the front room, I could read till late in the night. In the back room they would switch off the lamp; they would say my old eyes were too weak to read past midnight, I must rest, I must not go blind, I must see my grandson grow and marry and have many

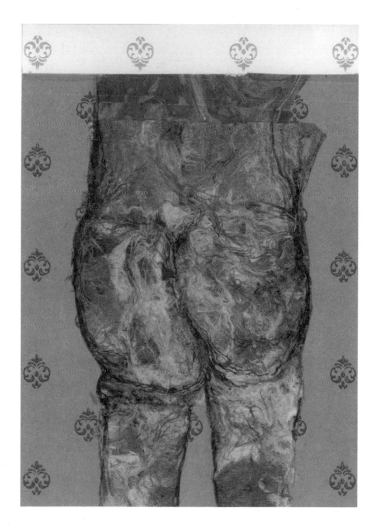

children. But my eyes were quickly forgotten as they carried out my torn, stained, lumpy mattress. "Whatever pleases you," they said, "we are here on earth to serve our elders." Hah!

In the front room, sometimes I read, but more often, after switching off the light, I go to the window. It has a cement ledge, nice and deep. I like sitting on it. Never for more than a few minutes, though. The cement is hard on my bones, on my shrivelled old arse of wrinkled skin-bags. Once, it was firm and smooth and bouncy. Once, it was a bum that both men and women enjoyed gazing after. Not so deep as a well, nor so wide as a church door – just the right size, and without blackheads or pimples. Firm and smooth and bouncy are the precisely operative words. Not bouncy like a Rubenesque young woman's, but enough, so that if you were to slap or squeeze it in a friendly fashion, both of us would feel good.

The cement is cool to the touch. You might think it a blessing in this hot climate. I don't. Not when I am craving warmth. Would you

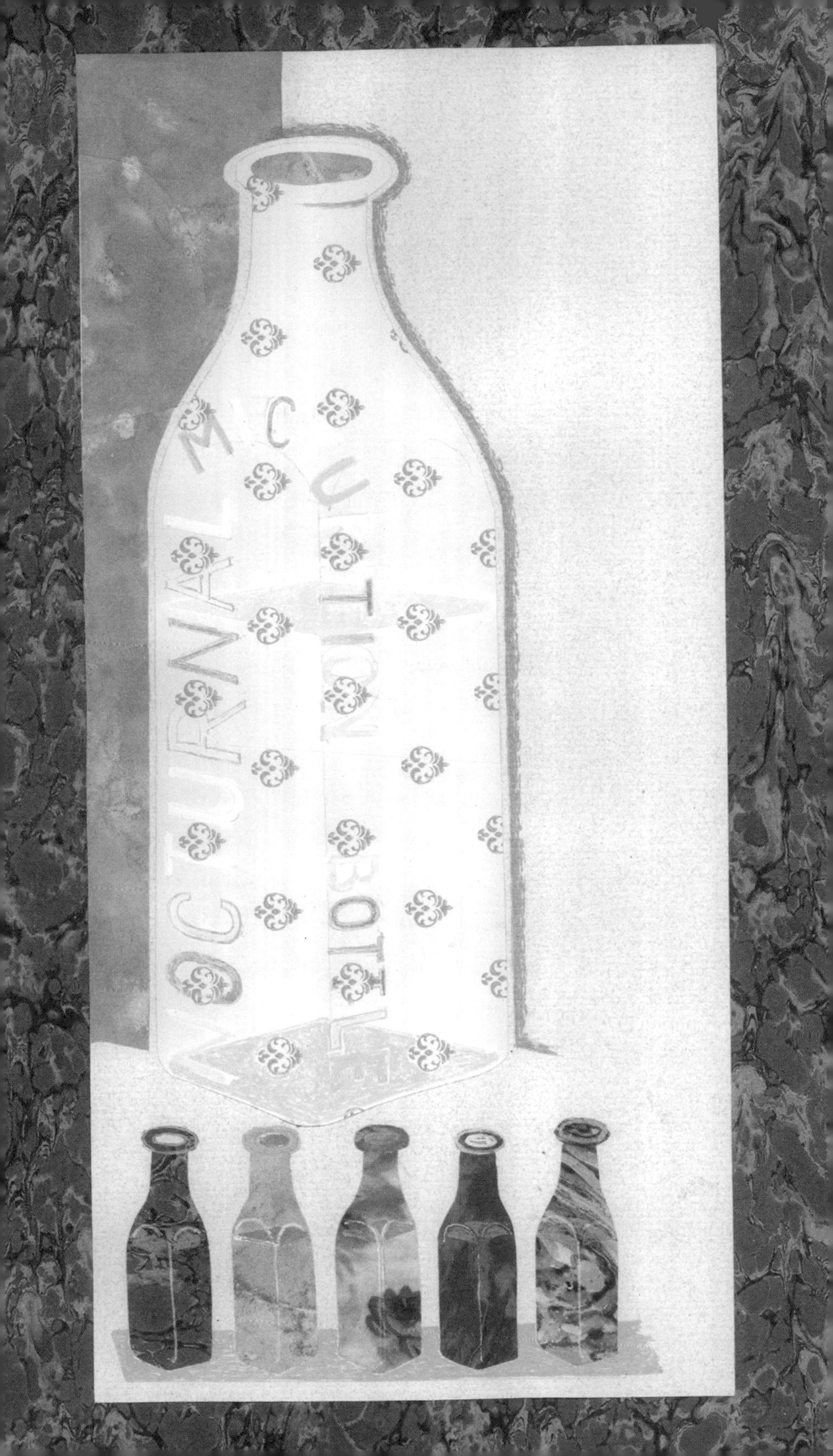
OCTURNAL M
C U TION
BOTTLE

believe me if I told you the ones in the back room chill the ledge with slabs of ice, to harass me?

But the window is convenient for making water at night. The water closet is through the back room; if I stumble past after the others are asleep, cursing and screaming follow me all the way. The neighbourhood dogs use the shrubs that grow outside my window. They do not mind me. My water is pure H_2O. Without smell, without colour. Nothing much left inside me, neither impurity nor substance.

I used to keep a milk bottle. I'd labelled it Nocturnal Micturition Bottle, so no one might utilize it after me for an incompatible purpose. The ones in the back room said the spelling was wrong, that it should be a-t-i-o-n, not i-t-i-o-n. Their audacity is immedicable. When they were little (and I was young), they used to ask me for meanings, spellings, explanations. I inculcated the dictionary habit in them. Now they question my spelling.

Like you. Yes, don't deny it. I see you reaching

for the OED. No need to be sneaky, do it with open pride, it is one of the finest acts. To know the word — its spelling, the very bowels of its meaning, the womb which gave it birth — this is one of the few things in life worth pursuing.

Something strange started to occur after I began keeping the milk bottle. The volume of water I passed increased night by night. One bottle was no longer enough. It would not surprise me if the others were slipping a diuretic into my food or medicine to torment me. Soon there were six milk bottles, duly labelled, standing in a row at the foot of my mattress each night. They were always full before the sun rose. At the crack of dawn, I emptied them down the toilet bowl. I felt a pang of loss. Was there no better use for it?

But one night, a bottle slipped through my fingers while micturating. Wet shards glinted murderously on the floor. For days together, the others went on about it. My hands keep shaking because of this disease that I have. They tell me there is no cure. Should I believe them?

The doctor said the same thing, granted. But how long does it take to bribe a doctor, slip him a few rupees?

The first night of the scream, I was not reading or sitting on the window ledge or micturating. I was asleep. Then the scream rose again in the street, the man begged for mercy. There was no mercy. He pleaded with them to be careful with his arm, that it would break. It only goaded them to more cruelty. He screamed again. Still no one awoke. Or they pretended not to.

Why do I have to listen to this, I asked myself. If only I could fall asleep again. So difficult, at my age. Oh, so cruel, finding sleep after long searching, only to have it torn away. And afterwards, my scourge of worries and troubles to keep me company. Trishul-brandishing sadhus agitating for a trade union. Vermilion-horned cows sulking, spurning the grass offerings of devotees. The snake charmer's flute enraging the cobra. Stubborn funeral pyres defying the kindling torch.

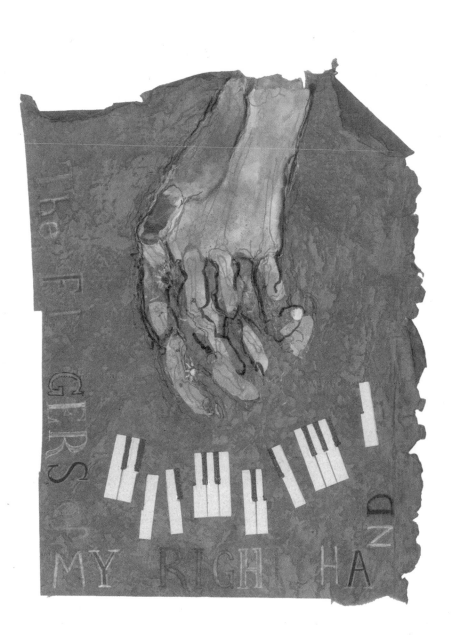

That night, I shivered and sweated, afraid to rise from between the sofa and the baby grand to look out the window. An upright would have made more sense than a baby grand in this tight space, I thought. Lying on the mattress, I could reach the pedals with my feet and lift my arms to tickle the ivories, joining distantly in the back-room orchestra of wind instruments.

Once upon a time, I took piano lessons. I practised on this very baby grand. After the second lesson my right-hand fingers were caught in the doors of the piano teacher's lift. Made from a mighty oak, they closed on my hand. I did not scream. When I retrieved my fingers, they were a good bit flattened. I smiled embarrassedly at my fellow passengers in the lift. There was no pain. My first thought was to restore the proper shape. I squeezed and kneaded the crushed fingers, comparing them to the undamaged left hand, to make sure I was achieving the correct contours. I could hear faint crunches. Then I fainted.

If I listen hard, I can hear those crunches of

my bone fragments even now when I flex my fingers. Flexed in time and rhythm, they resemble dim castanets — I can do the Spanish Gypsy Dance and Malagueña. These days, the only person who plays the piano is the servant boy. A piano for a servant, denying my mattress the floor space.

The other night a mouse ran over my ankles as I lay on the mattress. That was not unusual; almost every night a mouse brushes my hands or feet. But my feeling comforted by its soft touch was most disconcerting. Happily, the usual disgust and revulsion followed the pleasant sensation. I hated mice as a young man. I prefer to keep hating them as an old one. And the world stays a safer place.

Did you know, mice can nibble human toes without causing pain or waking the sleeper? The saliva of mice induces local anaesthesia and promotes coagulation, curbing excessive bleeding. Their exhaled breath, blown with expert gentleness on the digits in question, is quite soothing till the morning comes.

I tell the ones in the back room about my fears of murine amputation. They don't care. No doubt, they would be pleased if I woke up missing a few fingers or toes. They laugh at me. For them, whatever I say is a laughing matter, worthless rubbish. I am worthless, my thoughts are worthless, my words are worthless.

One day I lost my temper. "Floccinaucini-hilipilificators!" I shouted in their general direction. Not comprehending, they laughed again, assuming I had lapsed into the galimatias of senescence.

You seem very sensible, for not laughing. Doubtless, you have also run into a mouse or two. If the feeding habits of *Mus musculus* interest you, I could tell you more. We shall return to it presently.

The screams on the street gave way to groaning. There were muffled thuds, blows landing on unprotected parts. Diaphragm, kidneys, stomach. Groaning again, then violent retching. I trembled, I was sweating, I wished it would end. The air was parched. If only there were

thunder and rain. If there were screaming,
and also thunder and rain, it might be bearable,
I thought.

The mice leave the piano alone. They never
run over the keys or romp among the wires and
hammers. Still, I keep hoping to hear plinks,
plonks, and accidental arpeggios in the night.
Expectations created long, long ago by children's
stories, I suspect. They have turned out to be
lies, like so much else.

Flying cockroaches, for instance. They are not
half as terrifying as they were made out to be.
The secret is to keep a cool head when the
whirring approaches your face. First, arm
yourself with a slipper and stand still instead
of flailing; then, as its flight pattern becomes
predictable, kill it on the wing. Simple. I am
proud to do it so well at my age. Flying or non-
flying, cockroaches hold no fear for me. No, it is
the insidious mouse with its anaesthetic saliva
and soothing suspiration that I dread when
darkness falls.

Another night – not the one of the scream or

the soft and pleasing mouse — when, sleepless,
I looked out my window, a chanavala was
approaching from Chaupatty, from the beach,
his neck-slung basket poised before him, ready
to serve. I smelled quantities of gram and
peanuts in the basket. A tin can with its mixture
of chopped onions, coriander, chilli powder,
pepper, and salt, along with a slice of lemon,
added its aroma to the dry, rainless air. My
mouth was watering.

The ones in the back room have forbidden
me all spices. They say the masala causes a sore
throat, tonsilitis, diarrhoea; and the burden of
these sicknesses will fall on their heads, they
say. So they give me food insipid as my saliva.
And it always has too much salt or no salt at all.
Deliberately. In the beginning it made me a
little cross; I would yell and throw the dinner
about. Then I realized this was what they
wanted, to starve me to death An abrupt
change of tactics was called for. Now, the
worse the meal, the more I praise it. Their
disappointed faces, deprived of the daily

MEN

MUSCULAR

spectacle, are a sight. Of course they pretend to be glad that I am enjoying myself.

And their tricks do not stop at food. Even my medicine they deprive me of, ignoring the schedule prescribed by the doctor. Then, when my hands and feet shake violently, they point to them and say, "See how sick you are? Let us take care of you. Be good, listen to what we say."

Oh, wickedness. Oh, the tyranny of it. But I will get the better of them. One of these days they will forget to hide the key to my wardrobe. Then I will be dressed and gone to my solicitor before they can say floccinaucinihilipilification.

The silhouette of the chanavala and his neck-slung basket made me yearn for something. I could not identify the object of my yearning. He had a small wire-handled brazier to roast the peanuts. Charcoal glowed in the brazier. I wished I could reach through the window and feel the warmth of that ember.

The chanavala was accosted by three men. They jostled him viciously, though at first they

greeted him like a friend. They grabbed hand-
fuls of peanuts and sauntered off. When the
chanavala walked under a street lamp, I saw his
tears. It might have been sweat. He lifted a
hand to wipe his face. Once, my eyes were
strong. Clear was my vision, piercing my gaze.
Never a chance of confusing tears with sweat.

The men who sleep outside the tall building
across the road were awake, and witnessed the
assault. But they did not intercede on the poor
chanavala's behalf. Most of them are very
muscular fellows. They went about getting
ready for sleep as if nothing was happening.
They might have been right. It is hard, at my
age, to know if anything is happening.

Watching the muscular fellows is my
favourite pastime at the midnight hour. There
is always laughing and joking as they unroll
their sleeping bundles, strip down to their
underpants, and take turns to use the tap in
the alley beside the building. Pinching and
slapping, pushing and shoving, their playful
preparation for bed continues. Some share a

bedding with a friend, cuddling under a thread-
bare cloth, hugging and comforting. I know
what it is like, the yearning for comfort.
Sometimes a woman appears. She spends a
little time with each of them, then disappears.

Unlike the building I live in, the one across
the road includes many amenities: private
nursing home, accountant's office, horoscope
and astrology service, furniture store, restaurant,
auto shop. Lorries with various gods and slogans
painted on their sides arrive daily at the building. The muscular men load or unload furniture
and auto parts during the day. They are always
in high spirits as they work.

Sometimes the prime minister visits from
the capital to consult the astrologer about a
favourable time for introducing new legislation,
or an auspicious month for holding general
elections. Then the police cordon off the area;
no one passes in or out of the building. There
are long traffic jams. People who want to obtain
their rations, take children to school, give birth,
go to hospital, or see the latest film have to wait

till the prime minister has finished with the nation's business.

The men who own the lorries also beseech the astrologer for propitious hours. The muscular men do not quibble about this. On the contrary, they are grateful: when the business was owned by unbelievers who did not take necessary precautions, a huge crate slipped and killed one of their comrades.

If the stars forbid the loading of lorries, the muscular men sit and watch the traffic. Once, on just such an idle day, a beggar stole a bun from the restaurant's front counter display. The waiters gave chase, caught him, and slapped him around till the muscular men rescued him. Then a policeman ran up to deliver the obligatory law-enforcement blows. The sun was very bright and hot. I was not squeamish about watching. I am not frightened of physical pain inflicted on others. Especially if it is in moderation. And there was nothing excessive about this action. Not like the police in that very backward northeastern state,

poking rusty bicycle spokes in suspected criminals' eyes, then adding a dash of sulphuric acid.

The waiters took back the mangled bun. The muscular men produced a coin. They insisted that the beggar return to the restaurant and purchase the comestible with dignity. With tender concern they stood round him to watch him eat it.

But the muscular men never go to the rescue of the screamer. I do not understand it. Nor do I understand, given my unsqueamish nature, why I cannot endure the screaming any more, the cries which occur at intervals every night, after midnight. I am shivering, my sweat feels cold, my knees ache and my brow is feverish, I am running out of things like mice, cock-roaches, chanavalas to occupy my mind, the scream and pain keep displacing them. The neighbour's dog begins to bark.

Brownie begins to bark. Brownie is the brother of a dog called Lucky, who died of rabies. In the back room they are fond of dogs, but blame me for their not being able to keep one. I would trip over the dog, they say, I would trip and fall and break my bones, and the burden of my broken bones would land squarely on their unprotected heads, they say.

Sometimes, they borrow Brownie from next door, to play with him and feed him the bones they save at mealtimes. Nowadays, they won't let me suck the marrowbones. They snatch them from my plate for Brownie. Even my marrow-spoon has been hidden away. The reason? A tiny splinter might choke me, they say, their excuses ever ready for the eyes and ears of the world. They try to teach Brownie to shake hands. The crotch-sniffing cur is not interested. He sticks his snout in my groin and knocks my onions around, like a performing seal. Day by day, they hang lower and lower. Great care must be taken every time I sit. Oh, to have again a scrotum tight as a fresh fig. The indignities of old age. Shrinking cucumber, and enlarging onions. That's fate. That's the way the ball bounces.

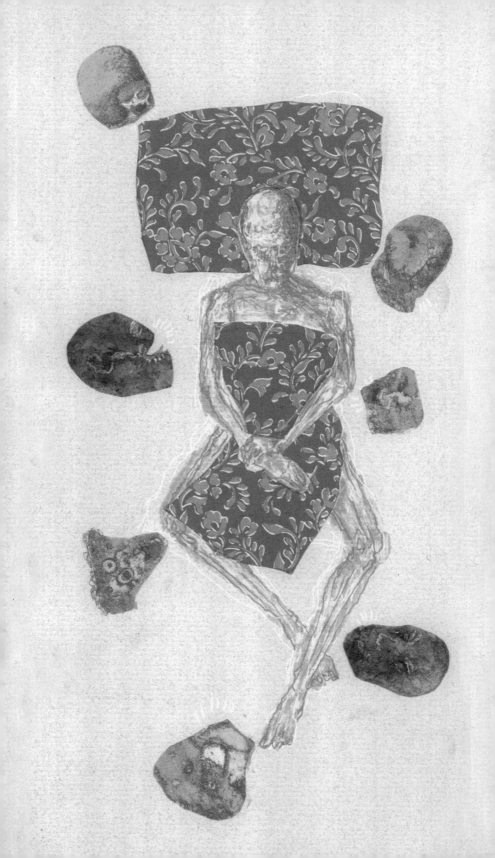

What destiny. Everything is my fault, according to the ones in the back room. They are so brave when it comes to subjugating an old man. No more nonsense about the scream, they warn me, it is all my imagination. Every day they tell me I have lost my mind, my memory, my sense of reality.

But wait. You be the judge. You weigh the evidence and form your opinion. Listen carefully to my words. Regard the concinnity of my phrasing. Observe the narrative coherence and the precise depiction of my pathetic state. Does this sound like a crazy man's story? Does it?

I implore you, plead my case with the ones in the back room. It is no more and no less than your duty. Apathy is a sin. This great age did not come upon me without teaching me virtue and vice. I speak the truth, I keep my promises. I am kind to the young and helpless. The young, I find, are seldom helpless.

Apathy is a sin. And yet, not one of them goes to help the screamer. How they can bear to

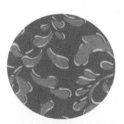

sleep through it, night after night, I don't know.
But what heroes they were, that morning, when
we found a harmless drunkard under the stairs.
He was sleeping like a baby, clutching to his
stomach a khaki cloth bag. There were three
hubcaps in the bag. Stolen, everyone proclaimed
at once. They shook him awake. Neighbours
came to look. They asked him questions. He
did not wish to answer. They kicked the desire
into him. When he answered, they could not
understand his thick-tongued mumbles. But
they have seen too many movies, so they kicked
him again. Blubbering, he explained he was a
mechanic, and produced a screwdriver from
his pocket as evidence. The murder weapon,
they shouted, and snatched it from him.
Someone suggested he might be dangerous.
So one of them got some string. It was the
flat kind, like a thin ribbon, with print on it:
Asoomal Sweets, Made Fresh Daily, it read.
They tied him with it, trussed him like a
stuffed bird. Oh, what heroes.

Not one dares to go out and look. The screams

keep coming. I weep, I pray, but the screams do not stop. I sleep with two pillows. One under my aching head, the other between my thighs. Some days I awake to an audience towering over my mattress and me. All the back-room heroes, standing there and laughing, pointing at the pillow between my withered thighs. I am silent then. I know the time will come when they too seek comfort in ways that seem laughable to others.

When the screams drive me over the edge of despair, when I am tired of weeping and praying, then I remove the pillow between my thighs and press it over my ears. Now the screaming stops.

In the morning I am neglected as usual while the back room comes to life. I open the curtain and look out. I scratch my pendent onions. Men go about their business. The sun is hot already. There is shame and fatigue on their faces. Lately, I have begun to see this shame and fatigue everywhere. The ones in the back room also wear it.

The dust is thicker today on the furniture.
I glance in the cold, pitiless mirror. The
reflection takes me by surprise: now I know
with certainty — if, perchance, the others have
not yet heard the scream, the time is not far
off. Soon it will rob them of their rest. Their
day will come. Their night will come. Poor
creatures. My anger is melting. All will be
forgiven.

The air is still dry, we wait for rain. The
beggars have gone on strike. The fields are sere,
the fishnets empty. The black marketeers have
begun to hoard. People are filling the temples.
The flies are dropping like men.

The illustrations for *The Scream* were done in what is often called mixed media. This term covers a multitude of approaches outside the tradition of, for example, oils, watercolours, pen and ink, acrylic. Mixed media can be non-specific and often embraces different techniques and materials, many of them not normally utilized in "fine art."

Although the story's setting is obviously India, the illustrations were conceived to be not "Indian" but rather to echo the richness of Indian miniatures and medieval manuscript illuminations, both of which I have admired for many years.

Some illustrations were begun in varying colours of tempera paint, a water-based paint with which you can go from the transparent to the opaque. They were then collaged over in certain areas with a variety of types of paper, some cut, some torn. I used marbleized paper (sometimes used for the endpapers of a book), wallpaper, and bark paper, enabling me to combine all sorts of rich colours and textures that traditional painting could not easily achieve. In addition to the tempera paint, I also used gel pens in order to give even more colour and richness to the works. The format of several illustrations is irregular where I thought appropriate, such as the broken fingers and the mattress.

A final note. All of the little "screaming heads" were literally "found" in one piece of marbleized paper, then enhanced ever so slightly with gel pens and carefully cut out with scissors and an exacto knife.

TONY URQUHART

September 2006

The publishers would like to acknowledge World Literacy of
Canada, who put together the idea for the collaboration between
Rohinton Mistry and Tony Urquhart that has resulted in this
book. Royalties from the sale of this book, donated by the
authors, will go directly to World Literacy of Canada to help
the organization continue its literacy work with women and
children in India.

For more on World Literacy of Canada, please contact:
401 Richmond Street West, Studio 236,
Toronto, Ontario, Canada, M5V 3A8
Telephone: 416.977.0008 Website: www.worldlit.ca
Email: info@worldlit.ca

A NOTE ABOUT THE TYPE

The Scream has been set in Walbaum. Originally cut by Justus
Erich Walbaum (a former cookie mould apprentice) in Weimar
in 1810, the type was revived by the Monotype Corporation in
1934. Although the type may be classified as modern, numerous
slight irregularities in its cut give this face its humane manner.

BOOK DESIGN BY CS RICHARDSON

ROHINTON MISTRY is the author of three novels, *Such a Long Journey*, *A Fine Balance*, and *Family Matters*, and a collection of short stories, *Tales from Firozsha Baag*. His fiction has won many prestigious awards in Canada and internationally.

TONY URQUHART is one of Canada's leading artists. His work has received major recognition at home and abroad, and he has played a crucial role in the development of contemporary art in Canada.